TITCHY WITCH

AND THE WOBBLY FANG

For Isobel Louise - welcome
R.I.

To Sarah and Sam
K.M.

ORCHARD BOOKS
338 Euston Road, London NW1 3BH
Orchard Books Australia
Level 17/207 Kent Street, Sydney, NWS 2000
First published in Great Britain in 2003
First paperback publication in 2004
This edition published in 2015
ISBN 978 1 40833 783 7
Text © Rose Impey 2003 Illustrations © Katharine McEwen 2003
A CIP catalogue record for this book is available from the British Library
1 3 5 7 9 10 8 6 4 2
Printed in China
Orchard Books is a division of Hachette Children's Books,
an Hachette UK company
www.hachette.co.uk

TITCHY WITCH

AND THE WOBBLY FANG

ROSE IMPEY ★ KATHARINE McEWEN

ORCHARD

Titchy-witch

Victor

Eric

Wendel

Weeny-witch

Witchy-witch

Cat-a-bogus

Titchy-witch had a wobbly fang.
It wibble-wobbled all the time
and she didn't like it. "Yuk!"

"Leave it alone," said Cat-a-bogus.
"It will come out when it's good
and ready."

But Titchy-witch couldn't wait
for that.

She and Dido tried to pull it out.

But the fang just wasn't ready.

Titchy-witch wanted a spell to
make it fall out.
But Dad was busy in his
workshop...

...and Mum said, "What would the Fang Fairy say?"

Titchy-witch didn't know about the Fang Fairy.

"When a fang comes out," Witchy-witch told her, "you put it under your pillow. Then, if you're good, the Fang Fairy brings you a surprise."

Titchy-witch loved surprises.

She wanted hers this minute.

She decided to make a spell
of her own.
"Come on, Dido," she said.
"This should be easy-breezy."

As soon as Mum was out of the way, she borrowed a few magic ingredients.

"Wasp's sting, beetle's wing,
Dragon's egg, lizard's leg,
Monkey's tail, slime of a snail,
Prickly thorn, unicorn's horn..."

Titchy-witch thought that should
be enough.

Dido thought it might be too much!

Then she said some special magic
words: "Hocus pocus,
          Bim Bala Bang
          Please pull out…"

16

Titchy-witch was about to say,
"this wobbly fang."
But she had an even better idea.

Mum said the Fang Fairy would bring one surprise present for each of her fangs.

How many presents would she bring for all her fangs?

Titchy-witch started again:

"Hocus pocus,
Bim Bala Bang
Please pull out
all my fangs..."

Clitter, clatter, clitter, clatter.
A whole set of little fangs fell out
and rolled round the kitchen floor.

Titchy-witch looked a bit funny
with no fangs.

Dido thought she looked
a bit scary.

But Titchy-witch wasn't too worried...

...until Cat-a-bogus called her for tea.

It was hard eating termites on toast without any fangs.

Titchy-witch was keeping very quiet too. The cat soon knew something was wrong.

Cat-a-bogus was mad. In fact, he
was furious.

He made Titchy-witch empty
her pockets.

Then the cat made some magic of his own. Most of the fangs went back.

All except one, which wibble-
wobbled a bit.
Then it kept on
falling out.

Next day, Titchy-witch found a shiny silver slovrin under her pillow. That would buy lots of chocolate grobblies.

And she still had lots more fangs
to go.

TITCHY WITCH

BY ROSE IMPEY ILLUSTRATED BY KATHARINE McEWEN

Enjoy a little more magic with all the Titchy-witch tales:

Orchard Books are available from all good
bookshops, or can be ordered from our website:
www.orchardbooks.co.uk
or telephone 01235 827702, or fax 01235 827703.

Prices and availability are subject to change.